THE
DIVORCE
PILL

Doug Bierl

ISBN: 978-1-7320425-0-6

Categories: Self help:
- Healthy Relationships
- Marriage
- Divorce
- Family Living

The Divorce Pill

Introduction

IT'S BEEN SAID that divorce is a bitter pill to swallow. What if there was actually a "divorce pill" that you could take that would let you experience what life would be like after divorce? If you were able to get a glimpse into the future, would it change your mind about divorce? Would you decide to move forward knowing the risks? Would you think your situation will be different from everyone else's?

We are in a society that often looks for a pharmaceutical solution for our ailments and to solve life's problems. We take a pill because it is easier and quicker than addressing the underlying issue. Some pills ease pain, improve mood, cure illness, or keep us from

i

doing bad things. Some are easy to swallow, and some are difficult.

Many times, we knowingly choose things that are not good for us. Sometimes, divorce is one of those things. Divorce has been around forever, although there was a time when it was less prevalent than it is today. Now, nearly every person in America is affected by divorce, either directly or indirectly. Divorce is common, accepted, and even expected. Long and successful marriages are becoming less and less common.

If you are reading this book, you may be struggling in your marriage or know someone who is. You may be at a point where divorce appears to be the only real option. You or your spouse may have resigned yourself to stay together for the sake of the children, but your heart is no longer in your marriage. Whatever the case, you're in for an experience of a lifetime!

Splitus (dexa-humanistic-choice hydrochloride), the "Divorce Pill," creates a hallucinatory 24-hour experience allowing a person to see and experience divorce in a very real way. The patient sees the future and experiences what life would be like after divorce. While under its affects, the patient experiences a virtual reality, and vividly remembers the hallucinations when the effects wear off. The events and situations that the patient experiences are based on what many couples go through after making the decision to divorce. Splitus allows patients to see what lies ahead after divorce.

The Divorce Pill was developed to help people to better understand all the implications of divorce on themselves, as well as their children, family, friends, co-workers, employer, and everyone else in their life. It is the drug manufacturer's hope, that with that knowledge, couples will decide that staying married is far more rewarding. If not, at least they will go into the divorce with more knowledge that may help them behave in a healthier way for all involved.

In this book, we present a case study of Brian Walker, one of the patients from a large clinic approved to administer Splitus. Through what you learn about him and what he experiences while under the influence of Splitus, you will undoubtedly see parallels in your life, or in the lives of others you know.

DISCLAIMER: The medicine and characters in this story are fictitious. Some of the situations are based on the personal experience of the author and others, but the circumstances have been changed to protect the identity of those involved.

The Candidate

BRIAN WALKER HAS been married to Lillie for 15 years. Both were raised Catholic and attend church regularly. They have three children, John (13), Peter (9), and Connie (6). Although a busy and hard-working financial advisor, Brian is a good father who goes to every sporting event, concert, play, and everything else his children do. Brian and Lillie would say that they have experienced the typical ups and downs most married couples go through. When people look at Brian, they see a supportive husband who cares for and encourages his wife, treating her with kindness and compassion. From outward appearance, the marriage looks good.

What nobody could see was that Brian had kept a secret, which Lillie uncovered one day. While cleaning out Brian's pants pockets as she was doing laundry, Lillie found a couple of crumpled receipts for a place she didn't recognize. That evening, Brian winced as the bedroom door slammed shut. Lillie had discovered the truth. He was having an affair. Lillie couldn't believe this was happening. Brian told her it was over and didn't mean anything. She didn't believe him. He didn't think she would get over the affair and wanted out of the marriage, but he hesitated because of the kids. He remembered hearing about a new drug that people called the "Divorce Pill" and the next day he applied to see if he was eligible to take it.

Eligibility Screening

ROMNEY HOSPITAL AND CLINICS, located in Outskirts, Ohio is the site of a major clinic authorized to administer a drug called Splitus (dexa-humanistic-choice hydrochloride), more commonly known as the Divorce Pill. This pill allows people to see what divorce might look like before they make their final decision. Splitus is administered in a controlled clinical setting, such as a hospital or sleep clinic while patients enter a 24-hour drug-induced sleep state where they experience vivid hallucinations of what their life would look like when divorced.

Splitus has been extremely revealing for those who have taken it. Stories of lives, marriages, and families transformed and restored have been making headlines all across the country. It has been hailed by many as a life-saving, marriage-saving miracle. Nearly everyone agrees that the Divorce Pill is a medical breakthrough with widespread impact. It has prevented thousands of divorces. Although only on the market a short time, divorce rates in the US have started to trend down since Splitus was approved.

People are clamoring to take this drug, flocking to pre-authorized clinical centers, including the one in this rural town. To be eligible, participants must have been married for at least five years and be contemplating divorce. They must be generally in good health and have no serious mental, heart, or liver conditions. Patients are

Dedication

To married couples who are experiencing challenges in their relationship and contemplating divorce, may this book be a stimulus to renew your commitment to stay married.

Acknowledgements

This book would not have been possible without the love, support, partnership, insight, and watchful eyes of my wife, Julaine.

Many thanks to my editor, Susan Sparks of ASAP Writing Services, for her guidance and patience through the rounds of revisions, especially after she thought we had made final changes.

Thanks to Dylan Menges of Menges Design for the cover illustration and design.

carefully screened through a detailed medical and personal history before being approved to receive the drug.

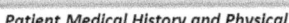

Patient Medical History and Physical

Patient : Brian Walker Gender: Male Age: 40
Occupation: CPA, Financial Advisor
Eyes: Brown Hair: Brown Height: 6 ft, 0 in Weight: 195 lbs
BP: 120/80 Temp: 98.6 Vision: 20/20 (with correction)
Hearing: Normal Allergies: None
Conditions: Depression Medications: Nortriptyline
Surgeries: None Hospitalization: None
Mother: Jane (Madison) Larrimer, age 60; healthy
Father: William Walker, age 65; high BP, elevated cholesterol
Siblings: Sally (Walker) Williams, age 37; no medical conditions
            Julie Walker, age 32; no medical conditions

Patient Personal History
Marital Status: Married 15 years, contemplating divorce
Spouse: Lillie, age 38
Occupation: Nurse
Children: John, age 13; Peter, age 9; Connie, age 6
Previous Marriages: None
Sexual History (self): Age 18: High school girlfriend, senior year (6 months);
Age 19: College Freshman year, two women (1 month, 3 months); Age 20:
Lillie: Age 36: Affair with business associate lasting 1 year
Spouse Sexual History: Age 20: Brian

Reason Considering Divorce
Lillie found out about her husband Brian's affair. He thought he was in love with his former mistress and remains in contact with her, but not sexually. She's single and 10 years younger than Brian. He doesn't feel in love with Lillie and they've talked about divorce, but he also doesn't want his kids to go through the breakup of their family. Even so, he thinks he's ready to take that step because he can't live with the guilt around his affair.

Based on the medical and personal history, Brian meets the eligibility criteria for administration of Splitus.

Brian is excited and a bit relieved when he gets the call. He's hoping the Divorce Pill will help him reach a decision once and for all.

Patient Intake
Saturday 8:00 am

BRIAN'S HANDS TREMBLE as he signs the consent form at the patient check-in desk. He's quickly greeted by Flo, the clinic nurse, who escorts him to his room. "I'll be your nurse while you are with us. Congratulations on being selected to receive Splitus. I've worked with a lot of patients and they all remark about the impact the experience has had on their life. Go ahead and change into this gown, put your personal items in the closet, and I'll be back momentarily."

Brian changes into the hospital gown and stows his valuables in the closet. He sits nervously on the edge of the bed, waiting for Flo to return. He notices a dark window and wonders if someone is behind it. Will they be watching him?

Pushing a small cart with a computer and several small wires attached, Flo knocks and then enters the room. "Alright Mr. Walker, here's what we're going to do. I will place these leads on your chest and head, which will allow us to monitor your vital statistics and brain wave activity. You see that mirror over there?" pointing to what looked like a dark window on the wall next to the bed. "Once we give you the drug, I will be back there with another staff member and we will be observing you for the 24-hour period after you take Splitus. We will record you while you are sleeping. We also use what we call the dream catcher, which lets us see what you are thinking and experiencing in your hallucinations.

Once we have hooked up the monitoring equipment, we'll give you Splitus, and you'll fall asleep within 30 minutes. You will stay asleep for 24 hours, during which time you will experience dreams about what your life will look like if you go through with your plans for divorce.

When you wake up, we will give you something to eat and you'll be able to shower and get dressed. Then, you will meet with a counselor to discuss and process your experience. That could take up to a couple of hours, depending on how much you need to process. Once you are finished with that, we'll send you home. If all goes well, you'll be having dinner with your family tomorrow night. Do you have any questions about anything?"

"I do have one question," Brian said. "I know that I will remember the dreams that I experience. Can you tell me about what the dream experience will be like?"

"Every patient is different," Flow answered. "The dreams will be very vivid and real, and you will easily remember them. For some patients, they can be disturbing because of what they see, and it may help to meet with a counselor for a few sessions after treatment. Most patients don't need that. The memory of the dreams will typically last for a year, but it could be longer. It depends in a large part on what happens in life that might trigger a flashback to the dream. Don't worry. Patients that have been followed for up to two years haven't had any serious problems."

Flo attaches the dream catcher and presents Brian with a blue and pink capsule. Within 30 minutes, he is sleeping soundly.

The Visions Begin
Saturday 10:00 am – The Betrayal

BRIAN TOSSES AND TURNS in his sleep while scenes play out on the dream catcher. Flo wondered what brought on Brian's desire for divorce. She scanned his file: Affair with a co-worker, Anita, 10 years younger than Brian. He said she caught his eye immediately; well-dressed, petite figure, and full of energy, the type of person who lit up the room.

It started while Brian was away at a business meeting. He and Anita first started talking during the group dinner. Before that, he noticed her in the office, but all that they had exchanged were passing glances and polite greetings. During the dinner, the conversation was easy, and Brian really connected with her. He hadn't felt this way since his early years with Lillie. After dinner, the group went to a nightclub for some drinks and dancing. Anita and Brian drank and danced a lot that night, including several slow dances where they looked deeply into each other's eyes.

Coming back to the hotel, Brian walked Anita to her room. Along the way, he held her hand and as they came up to the door, put his arms around her, pulled her close, and they kissed. She didn't resist, and their lust for each other grew increasingly intense. She opened the door and they worked their way in, threw off each other's clothes and had sex late into the night. As Brian left Anita's room, he couldn't believe what just happened. He thought about Lillie and guilt set in.

Flo thought, *I guess the guilt didn't last too long!* The record shows that when they returned from the meeting, Brian couldn't stop thinking about Anita. The first day back in the office, Anita sent an email to Brian to let him know how much she enjoyed their time together and how she hoped they could continue seeing each other. She knew that Brian was married, but said that it didn't matter to her. Brian and Anita continued to meet secretly on a regular basis for about a year. Anita fell in love with Brian and said he needed to choose between Lillie and her. Brian was torn. While he felt love for Anita, he also didn't want to put his kids through divorce. He told Anita that he couldn't do it and they broke off the relationship. Furious, Anita threatened to tell Lillie, but never went through with it. She couldn't deal with seeing Brian at the office, so she went to work for another company. But, Brian couldn't stop thinking about her and it wasn't long before he would contact her again.

"Well, I guess he must be ready to make that change, or at least he thinks he is. Let's see what's going on with Brian now." Flo gestured to her associate to look at the dream catcher screen again.

Saturday 11:00 am – Revenge!

A NEW SCENE CAME into focus. Brian was in a rather heated discussion with Lillie. Brian shouted, "I can't believe you did this! I told you it was over between Anita and me and that I broke it off with her. I told you that I wanted to keep our family together. So why did you have to go and have an affair?"

"Sure, you said that you broke it off, but I could tell that you didn't really want to. You just did it because of the kids. It didn't have anything to do with loving me. You didn't even tell me that you wanted to stay with me. So, I wanted to see how *you* would feel if I slept with someone else," Lillie shot back. "But, I couldn't even bear the guilt of a one-night-stand and so I had to tell you. It didn't mean anything to me. It's not like I even know the guy. I just picked him up at a bar. I had to get drunk to even let it happen. The only pleasure I got out of it was in knowing that it would hurt you."

"You're damn right it hurts me! I choose to stay with you and work out our marriage and you go and do something like this. I can't believe it!" Brian snapped.

"You only *said* that you wanted to work things out, but what have you done? You went to *one* counseling session and then said it wasn't helping! You didn't even give it a chance! You haven't even said you're sorry for being unfaithful! I don't think I can take this any longer," Lillie sobbed.

"Fine! Then, let's just end it now," Brian fired back. "It's clear to me that we'll never be able to work things out. I'm finished trying. We can tell the kids tomorrow, after dinner."

He stormed away mumbling, *she's ungrateful and doesn't appreciate what I'm trying to do. I can call Anita and enjoy life with her. I can't stop thinking about her anyway, and I bet she would take me back. Life will be so much better without Lillie constantly being on my back.*

The scene changes again.

Saturday 12:00 pm – The Break Up

BRIAN IS SITTING in a kitchen with Lillie. It is evening and it looks like they have just finished dinner. They move to the family room where John, Peter, and Connie are watching television. Brian turned off the TV and began to address them.

"Kids, your mom and I have something important to tell you. We need you to listen real carefully. We have some issues that we can't work through, so we've decided to get a divorce. Now, I know this may be hard to understand, but we've decided that it's what we need to do.

We want you to know that we both love all of you more than anything and we will still be your mom and dad. We'll just be living in different houses. You will stay here with mom, and you'll come to visit and spend time with me where I live. Do you have any questions?"

Peter and Connie started crying as Brian shared this news. Connie asked, "But Dad, why do you have to get a divorce? Can't you just work things out? We'll be better and help out more around the house. We'll be good."

"Connie, you and the boys haven't done anything wrong," Brian said softly. "This is a grown-up thing between your mom and me."

"Sweetheart, your dad and I love you very much," Lillie chimed in. "This is not about you."

John spoke up, "It may not be about us, but we are affected too. Why do you need to do this to us? Everything is just fine the way it is. I don't want to be like other kids I know who go between their mom and dad's. This sucks!"

Peter then joined the conversation. "Dad, where will you live?"

"In a few days, I will move into an apartment," Brian explained. "You'll come to see me on Monday and Wednesday evenings, and then stay the night with me on Friday up until dinner time on Saturday. That way, I'll get to see you and spend time with you every week."

Flo watched another scene come into focus on the dream catcher. Brian had just dropped off the kids and was driving away from the house. He stopped alongside the road and started crying. "What have I done? These kids are the best things that have happened to me and I'm tearing them apart. How did I let things get this bad? Why should they pay the price for my bad choices? They don't deserve this!"

Saturday 1:00 pm – The Legal Battle

BRIAN AND LILLIE ARE in a small courtroom, each seated at separate tables with an attorney. A judge is seated on the courtroom bench in front of them. "Mr. and Mrs. Walker, I grant your motion to dissolve your marriage. Mrs. Walker will be the custodial parent and Mr. Walker will have regularly scheduled visitation as the two of you agreed. Mr. Walker, you will pay spouse support until your youngest child is eighteen. It is due regardless of your income and it will only stop if Mrs. Walker remarries. In addition, you will pay child support until each child reaches the age of eighteen or graduates from high school, whichever comes later. This amount is due regardless of your income as well. Mrs. Walker will retain the marital house and become its sole owner. She will also receive half of the liquid assets and half of the current value of Mr. Walker's retirement plan. Do you both understand and accept what you are agreeing to?"

Brian and Lillie nod in agreement. The judge declared their marriage dissolved and dismissed the court.

As Brian left the courtroom, he turned to his attorney. "I can't believe it's finally over. I thought it would never end. This has been going on for over a year. I've seen a side of Lillie that I never thought existed. She dug up as much dirt on me as she could and the judge fell for it hook, line, and sinker. She made me look like a real jerk," he complained. "She's taken me to the cleaners and I don't know how I'm going to have a life after I pay the court costs, legal fees, spouse support, and child support. I can't even remember why I married her. I can't stand to be around her now. But, I still have to go through her to talk with my kids and see her every time I pick them up."

Saturday 2:00 pm – Divided Celebrations

BRIAN IS WITH HIS father, mother, sisters, and their families for Thanksgiving dinner. He addressed the group, "I miss having my kids here. It really stinks that they can't be with me every holiday. I'm not crazy about having assigned holidays. Lillie has them for Thanksgiving. I get them for Christmas Eve. She gets them for Christmas day. We alternate every other holiday and then switch the following year. It means that I never really get to celebrate holidays with them. We even alternate birthdays every other year. Of course, when one of the kids has something special going on, all hell breaks loose!"

Saturday 3:00 pm – Outlaws And Old Friends

CONNIE, WEARING A PRETTY white dress, is surrounded by a backyard full of people. Brian hugged her and said, "Honey, I'm so proud of you! How does it feel having celebrated your First Holy Communion?"

"Okay, I guess," Connie shrugged. "I don't feel any different, except that now I'll be able to go to Communion with the boys and Mom on Sundays, or with you when we go to Mass together."

13

Brian smiled and jokingly replied, "Well, it's a big day for me because it's just another sign that my little girl is growing up. This is your first step to becoming a full member of the church. Before you know it, you'll be getting married!"

"Dad! Yuk! I don't even like boys." Connie squirmed.

As Brian was talking with Connie, he overheard a conversation between Lillie's brother and sister. Her sister said, "I don't know why Lillie even invited him. He's a real jerk and he's made a real mess of her life. Have you heard about how he's been trying to get the kids to live with him?"

"I feel sick to my stomach just seeing him here," Lillie's brother replied. "Part of me wants to go up to him and give him a piece of my mind, and then some! Out of respect for Lillie and the kids, I won't."

Brian looked around the yard. He got the sense that all eyes were on him and that everyone was talking about him. Just then, he spotted one of his old friends and walked over to him.

"Hi Jim. I haven't seen you in quite a while." Brian said, extending his hand.

"I'm sorry about that," Jim replied. "Since you and Lillie split, I didn't know what to do. I really love both of you and I felt if I called you, I'd be betraying her. Besides, I almost never see you around anymore. I don't see you at church or in the neighborhood, so we don't have a chance to stay in touch. It's a really awkward situation, you know."

Brian nodded his head, "I guess it is, but I'd still like to get together with you sometime. Maybe we can play golf or go bowling. We used to do that, and it would be great to do it again."

"We'll see," Jim hesitated. "Well, I need to congratulate Connie. I'll be seeing you around." As Jim walked away, Brian looked around, feeling out of place. He had a few brief conversations and then hugged each of his kids, thanked Lillie for inviting him, and left.

Flo turned to her colleague, "Wow! Talk about a cold shoulder. Brian was really out of place in that party! Haven't we seen this time and time again?" Her colleague nodded in agreement. "It's such a shame," Flo groaned. "Once the divorce takes place, the relationship between the ex and former in-laws, or out-laws as I like to call them, usually breaks as much, or more than the relationship with the ex-spouse. The out-laws dig up all the dirt on the ex and have such disdain for him or her, but none of it ever came up before. I guess that's just their way of protecting their kin. Well, this exchange was mild compared to some of the ones we've seen. I mean, I've seen some fist fights at parties like this! It can get real ugly!"

Saturday 4:00 pm – On The Job

BRIAN IS AT HIS desk at work. He and his boss are having a meeting. "Brian, I know you are going through a tough time right now with the divorce and all. I've tried to be understanding and patient with you. When you were going through the divorce and needed time off to be with the kids, go to counseling, meet with the lawyers, and go to court, I gave you all the time you needed without question. But, it's been over a year since your divorce was final and your productivity still hasn't returned to what it was before the divorce. Half the time, you come in here late, looking disheveled, you miss key deadlines, you're in a bad mood a lot, and you're short with the staff. You need to get your act together. Maybe you need to get laid!"

That's what got me into this mess, Brian thought. "I'm doing the best I can to keep up with the kids, take care of my house and bills, deal with Lillie, and show up here every day. I know I haven't been as productive as before, but I'm still getting the work done."

His boss shot back, "Yes, you are completing the work. But, the quality of the work is not up to standards. You're not paying attention to the details. I find myself reviewing your work more closely and having to correct errors. Your clients also see it and they are starting to complain. I'm sorry to do this, but I'm going to have to put you on an action plan. If you don't show improvement in these areas within the next 90 days, I'll have no choice but to let you go. I don't want to do that and I'm here to support you in every way possible. You've always been a strong contributor and I want you to succeed." The two shook hands then Brian's boss left his office.

Brian closed the door, went back to his desk, dropped his head in his hands and started to cry. "What have I done? I have ruined my marriage, torn apart my family, disrupted the lives of my children, and now, I may lose my job! I didn't think it would be like this. I thought that Anita and I would be living together and having the time of our lives. But, by the time I made a decision, she had moved on to some guy more her age. So, now I'm alone. I'm struggling to pay my bills. Any free time I have is spent with the kids or in front of the TV with a drink in hand. I stay up late because I can't get to sleep. My life really sucks!"

"I feel sorry for him, but we see this so often," Flo commented. "Men and women who come in here have this distorted picture of what life is like after divorce. Then, they experience things like this and get a dose of reality. Some of them choose to ignore it and think this is not really going to happen to them, thankfully most take this as a wakeup call and change their ways. This pill is such a great discovery!"

Saturday 5:00 pm – Children In The Middle

BRIAN IS IN A RESTAURANT having dinner with John, Peter, and Connie when John catches Brian by surprise, "Dad, why are you and Mom always fighting?"

"Well, John, we just disagree on a lot of things, including how often I can see you," Brian said. "I am grateful that I can see you several days a week, but sometimes it's just not enough for me. Don't you want to see me more often too?"

The kids all nod in agreement.

Connie interrupts, "Mom wants to see us too and we want to be with her. We want to be with both of you, like we used to when you were married."

"Well, things are different now," Brian responded. "We all need to get used to our new normal."

"All of this isn't fair," Connie pouted.

"You know, if you let your mom know that you want to spend more time with me or even be with me the same amount of time as with her, I bet she would change," Brian said slyly. "Maybe you can even suggest that the time should be more equal. After all, that's the only fair thing, isn't it?"

Flo shook her head at the screen, "We see this kind of thing a lot, don't we? Every time, my heart goes out to the kids. They are caught in the middle of their parents' tug-of-war over their time, love, and affection, or over possessions or anything else that their parents don't want to give up. A lot of times, it doesn't even seem to be about the kids; it's more about pride. One parent doesn't want to let the other parent win or give the appearance that they have done so. It's so sad that it comes to this. Well, maybe this experience will give him a change of heart."

Saturday 6:00 pm – Dating Again

ANOTHER SCENE COMES into view on the screen. Brian is walking into a restaurant. He's greeted by the hostess and says, "I'm meeting a woman here and am a few minutes late. Do you know whether you've seated her?" Just then, a woman taps Brian on the shoulder. "Hi, I'm Mandy. You must be Brian."

Brian turns to see an attractive woman with long brown wavy hair, and eyes that seemed to look right into his heart and make it jump. She appears to be about his age. He stumbles for the words, "Yes, I am. I'm pleased to meet you. I'm sorry I'm late."

"It's okay. I just got here myself," Mandy smiled.

The hostess seated them at a small table near the back. The two carried on a conversation from the time they sat down until the waitress brought the check. Mandy is divorced as well, with three children, and she shares custody with their father. She works as a legal secretary at a small law firm. At the end of the evening, Brian told her that he'd like to see her again and she said she'd like that. They hugged and went to their separate cars.

Brian smiled to himself as he walked to his car. *I've finally met someone that I have something in common with and that I enjoy being around. I'm tired of friends setting me up with the 'perfect woman' or going on blind dates from the internet, or hanging out at a bar in the hopes of finding the right woman. I hope she had a good time with me. She seemed to, so maybe this is the start of something good. I just don't want to mess up again like I did with Lillie.*

Saturday 7:00 pm – Kids or Girlfriend?

BRIAN IS ON THE PHONE in his bedroom while John, Peter, and Connie are in the next room, watching

TV. "Mandy, I want to spend more time with you, I really do. But, I also feel torn. Since the separation, I've always had the kids for two days a week and one overnight. I really don't want to change that schedule. They need the consistency and I need to feel like I'm involved in their lives. I feel like you're making me choose between you and them."

He listened to Mandy's frustration and then continued, "Of course I want to be with you and I know that the days Bill has your kids don't match the days that I have mine. I know that makes it hard for us to have much time alone."

Mandy continued complaining about the arrangement and Brian snapped, "Well, what if you talk with Bill about changing your schedule to match mine? Yes, I know he's unreasonable and that he'll probably give you a hard time. But, his visitation is only one night a week and every other weekend, so it seems like it will be less of a change. If you can at least get the weeknight to match one of mine, then that will allow us to do things together with all the kids sometimes, and then we'll still have the evenings I'm not with my kids when I can come over, and half of the weekends when you don't have your kids. I also think..."

As Flo watched the scene, she turned to her colleague and said, "This is probably one of the most difficult things that happens after a divorce when people start dating again, especially when both have children and different visitation schedules. Neither one wants to change the schedule because it means they have to work it out with their ex, yet in most cases, one of them gives up time with their kids. And it doesn't always get any better when they get remarried. There seems to be a constant battle around visitation, even after all the legal papers are signed."

Suddenly, the screen flashes to another scene.

Saturday 8:00 pm – Married Again

BRIAN IS STANDING at an altar with Mandy in a small church. John, Peter, and Connie are there, along with three other children. About 50 people applaud as the minister said, "Let me introduce to you Mr. and Mrs. Brian Walker."

"I guess Brian and Mandy hit it off after that first date," Flo mused. "Those three other children must be hers. They look like such a nice couple and they seem to have the support of many family and friends." The scene continued with Brian and Mandy relaxing beside a pool.

Brian turned to Mandy, "I can't believe we're finally married. I'm so happy that you agreed to be my wife. I feel like I've been given a second chance with you."

Sipping her drink, Mandy replied, "I feel that way too. I didn't think I would ever find anyone else to love after Bill left me. You know how hard it was for me to get close to you when we first met. To think that just two years later, we are married. Amazing! I'm lucky to have found you, or should I say, that you found me. Jenny, Julie, and Sam are lucky to have you as their stepfather too. You are such a good influence for them."

"I hope I can be a good father figure for them," said Brian. "I sometimes question whether I have been to my kids."

The scene changes again.

Saturday 9:00 pm – Lillie Spirals Downward

LILLIE IS IN A HOSPITAL emergency room and Brian is standing next to her bed. The doctor turns to Brian explaining, "Mr. Walker, it seems that your ex-wife tried to commit suicide. She took half a bottle of sleeping pills and nearly succeeded, but your daughter found her and called 911. When she got here, we pumped her stomach and stabilized her. It appears that she will be okay, but she'll need to undergo an extensive psychiatric evaluation."

"I had no idea she was feeling this way," Brian exclaimed. "What will happen to her?"

The doctor answered, "That will be determined by the psychiatrist. She may need to undergo further treatment, or she may need to be institutionalized for a while, depending on how serious the situation is. We won't know until she wakes up and is examined further."

Brian remembered a discussion with the children that he had a few months before and the scene suddenly shifts again.

Saturday 10:00 pm –The Children Voice Concern

THE CHILDREN ARE WITH their dad in a small apartment, sitting around a table eating dinner. John is quickly consuming his meal, while Peter and Connie pick at their food. "Dad, Mom's been acting a little weird lately," Connie said. "She's forgetful a lot. On Tuesday, she almost forgot to pick up Peter at school."

"Yeah, and she seems to lose track of time and we're almost always late for things," Peter added.

With a mouth half full of food, John mumbled, "Not only that, but she seems to be sleeping a lot more than she used to, and she doesn't go out much. Heck, sometimes we don't even have enough food to eat in the house and she picks dinner up at a fast food place. Don't get me wrong, I love eating that stuff, but it's just different than it used to be."

Brian tried to downplay the situation. "Well, your mom is probably just going through a difficult time right now. I'm sure she'll be fine. Besides, she's doing the best she can to take care of you. It can't be all that bad."

Saturday 11:00 pm – A Change for the Children

THE HOSPITAL SCENE COMES back into focus. Once again, the doctor is talking with Brian, "Mr. Walker, since there wasn't another adult in the house when the ambulance arrived, and your children are minors, Children's Services has taken them into custody pending further investigation. I'm sure if you call them, they'll give

23

you temporary custody until things can be figured out. Here's their number." The doctor handed a card to Brian.

Brian paced frantically in the hospital hallway talking on his cell phone. "My wife took an overdose of sleeping pills and I was told that you have my kids in custody. I'd like to pick them up. Yes, I have a place for them to stay. Since our separation, they've been coming over two evenings and one overnight every week. Great, I'll be there in 15 minutes." Brian raced to his car, abruptly backed out of the parking space, and burned rubber as he sped away. He pounded on the steering wheel cursing every stoplight. *What in the world is happening here? What was Lillie thinking? What have we done to the kids?* Brian hurried into Children's Services, a cold, stark building with pale yellow walls.

"I'm Brian Walker and I'm here to pick up my children, John, Peter, and Connie," he stated.

"Take a seat," said the woman at the desk.

After what seemed like an eternity, a woman and his three children walked through the door. "I'm sorry you had to go through this," Brian cried, hugging the three of them close. "I had no idea things were this bad."

While in the car, Peter asked, "Dad, what's going to happen to Mom?"

"Well, she is going to be okay," Brian assured him. "She's sleeping right now. When she wakes up, the doctors will talk with her and do some more tests. She may have to have some treatment for a while. We'll know more in a few days."

"So, what are we going to do until then? What's going to happen to us?" Connie cried.

"You will live with me for now until we know more," said Brian. "Don't worry. I'll take care of you. If things don't get better with your mom, you'll just live with me."

Just then, he remembered that he hadn't called Mandy. He picked up his cell phone and after a few seconds said, "Honey, it's me. Yes, everything is okay, but I'm coming home with the kids. I'll explain more when we get home and we can talk then. We'll be home shortly. I'll stop and pick up some pizza on the way. Okay, I love you."

Sunday 12:00 am – A New Family Forms

WHILE LYING IN BED, Mandy turned to Brian. "I don't know if I can handle this. Ever since Lillie tried to kill herself and your kids came to live with us, it's just been crazy around here. We don't have enough space and it's always noisy. We don't have any time together and it seems like we're constantly running someone somewhere. Between that, my job, and having to deal with my ex-husband and my own kids, I just don't know if I can do it."

Brian flinched. "I hear what you're saying, and it hasn't been easy over the last three months, but what choice do I have? These are my children; the courts have determined that Lillie is an unfit mother. Given her mental state and what she tried to do, the courts won't even *think* about giving custody back to her. At this point, I'm not sure I would even let that happen."

"Don't I have any say in this?" Mandy retorted.

"Of course you have a say, but what choice do we have?" Brian asked. "Am I supposed to let some stranger raise my kids, or send them to someone else in the family? I'm their father and it is my responsibility to take care of them. I love them and don't want someone else to raise them. What kind of father would I be if I let that happen? Mandy, I know you didn't sign up for this when you agreed to marry me. I had no way of knowing that something like this would happen and would not have imagined it in my wildest dreams. But, since it has happened, I need you to stand beside me and work through it with me. Will you do that for me?"

With tears in her eyes, Mandy replied, "I guess I really don't have much of a choice. I love you and I love my kids. I'm growing to love your kids, too. But, this just may be too much for me to handle so suddenly. If it's going to work, you need to be around more often. You need to cut back on work hours and share the load. I think we also need to have the kids pitch in around here more. We need to assign chores to each of them and give them responsibilities. Are you willing to do these things?"

Brian pulled her close, "Yes. We have to adjust to the situation. I'll talk with my boss tomorrow and see what I can work out. Let's spend some time tomorrow night figuring out a chores list and schedule. Since John is driving now, he can help out with some of the shuttling of kids to and from activities. This weekend, we'll map it all out for the kids and discuss it with them. How does that sound to you?"

Reluctantly Mandy nodded in agreement. Then she looked up at Brian and said "It's hard for me to remember what life was like before all of this happened. It seems like so long ago."

Sunday 1:00 am – Battle with the "Ex"

BRIAN BLINKED IN SURPRISE as his office door suddenly flung open. A rather large man was in his face. "You think you're slick, don't you? Who do you think you are, not letting me talk to my kids? I knew you were going to cause problems when you married Mandy. If you try to keep me from my kids, I'll beat the living crap out of you!"

Shaken, Brian responded, "I'm not trying to keep you from your kids, but when you call after they are in bed..."

"I'll call whenever I damn well please," the man shouted. "They're my kids and if I want to wake them up and talk with them at midnight, you'd better let me. It's my right as their father! If you try to stop me, you'll pay."

"You know..." Brian started nervously.

"Yeah, I know. I know just the kind of person you are!" the man continued.

"You don't know anything about me." Brian shot back.

"I know enough. Just try to keep me from my kids again, and you'll be sorry." The man stormed away.

Brian closed his office door and pounded his fist on the desk, *I hate this. Who does he think he is, barging in here and threatening me? He's a real piece of work.* Brian picked up the phone, punching in Mandy's number. "Mandy, your ex just paid me a visit and threatened me. You know, I don't know how much more of this I can handle. He's a real jerk!"

"What did Bill say?"

"He said that if I try to keep him from your kids, he'll beat the crap out of me. He has a problem with us not letting him talk with the kids when he calls late at night. I'm just trying to do what you want."

"He just doesn't get it," Mandy agreed. "He thinks we should just drop everything we're doing and let him disrupt our lives whenever he wants to. He can be a royal pain at times. Do you want me to talk with him at the parent-teacher conferences tonight? You know he'll be there, showing up as the model father. He's really good about putting the charm on people, but watch out if you ever cross him!"

Sunday 2:00 am – Tensions at School

BRIAN IS WITH MANDY and her ex-husband, Bill, in a classroom with Mandy's son's teacher, who is talking with the three of them, "I'm concerned about Sam. Over the last few months, he has been kind of withdrawn. He seems distracted in class and he isn't completing many of his homework assignments. Has anything happened recently that might have caused it?"

Mandy cleared her throat, "Well, Brian and I got married just after the school year began and Sam has had a difficult time adjusting to the change. Plus, he splits his time between his dad and me, so he may not be in any kind of routine."

Bill added, "I know when he's with *me* I sit down with him every night and make sure he's doing his homework. I want him to do well in school. He's a smart kid. I know he's complained to me about living with his mom and step-dad and his three kids. I think there's a lot of tension between them."

"I'm not sure that's the problem," snapped Mandy. "Sure, there's some tension, but it's no more than normal sibling rivalry that goes on between Sam and his sisters. Maybe a bigger issue is the constant bickering between you and me. I know that upsets Sam a lot and he probably feels torn between the two of us."

Bill fired back, "Well, if you'd stop telling him how bad I am, maybe that would help!"

"Hold on a minute," the teacher interrupted, "Let's not lose sight of why we're here. We need to put differences aside and focus on Sam, and what's in his best interest. Now, let's discuss what we might do to work on the areas where he's struggling."

Brian sat quietly, feeling like a third wheel while the parent-teacher conference continued.

Sunday 3:00 am – Step-Fighting

JENNY YELLED, "Moooommm! Peter won't let me have the remote so that I can watch my show!"

Mandy and Brian entered the family room together and Mandy asked, "What's going on here?"

"I'm watching a football game and Jenny came barging in here demanding that I give her the remote," Peter explained. "She thinks she owns the TV!"

"I *always* watch *Teen Idol*!" Jenny shouted.

Brian looked at both of them and said, "Well, if the two of you can't work this out, then neither of you will watch the show. Give me the remote."

Peter got up and as he tossed the remote to his dad, he said, "I hate it here. I don't see why I need to share with her. She's not even my sister!"

Mandy responded, "Now, hold on a minute. Who do you think you are, talking to your father like that?"

"You're not my mom! You can't tell me what to do!" Peter said loudly.

Brian interrupted, "Mandy, let me handle this. Peter is my son and I need to take care of this." He grabbed Peter by the arm as he headed up the stairs.

"Peter, I don't appreciate you taking that tone with me and it is not acceptable for you to talk that way to Mandy. Like it or not, we are a family now and Jenny is your sister. You need to learn to share with her. Mandy may not be your mom, but she *is* your step-mother and you need to show her some respect. Do I make myself clear?"

"Sure, but this whole thing sucks!" He answered as he pulled his arm out of Brian's grip, and stomped up the stairs. Brian looked on and let him go.

Sunday 4:00 am – Discipline

"HOW AM I SUPPOSED to get any respect, if you don't let me handle the situation?" Mandy asked.

Brian answered, "I thought I needed to take care of Peter and I couldn't let him talk to you like that. He's my son and I need to be the one to discipline him."

"So, what you're saying is that you discipline your kids and I discipline mine, right?" Mandy demanded. "Then, how are we ever going to be parents to all of our children? We're never going to be a family if we do that! We're going to send the signal that one of us doesn't have any authority over the other's children. I think the kids will use that against us and play you against me or me against you. We need to come up with a better solution."

Brian sighed. "How can I have any authority over Jenny, Julie, and Sam, when anytime I discipline them or do anything to try to be a parent, they run off and tell Bill? Then, he tells them that they don't have to listen to me. At least you don't have to deal with that, since Lillie is pretty much out of the picture. What do you propose we do?"

"Let's call a family meeting and lay it out for them," Mandy suggested. "I'll make it clear that when my kids are here, you and I both have authority to parent them, regardless of what their father tells them. When

31

they are with him, he is the parent. You can tell your kids the same thing. We can answer any questions they have and then tell them that this is now a closed issue and we expect them to obey both of us. How does that sound?"

"I guess it's worth a shot," Brian conceded.

The dreams continued, wave after wave.

Sunday 6:00 am –Visitation Tug-of-War

BRIAN IS STANDING BEHIND Mandy at the front door as she talks with her ex-husband, Bill. Bill said, "Mandy, I'd like to take the kids to the zoo next weekend. I asked them if they wanted to go and they said that they'd really like to do that. I can pick them up Saturday morning around 10 o'clock and have them back by supper time. Okay?"

"Absolutely not!" snapped Mandy. "It's my weekend to have them, not yours. If you want to do things like that, you should plan them when you have them for the weekend. Last month, you wanted to take them to the park. The month before that, you just wanted to hang out with them. Why are you always asking to see them outside of normal scheduled visitation?"

Bill responded, "I want to spend time with them and they want to spend time with me. You see them a lot more than I do. Besides, when I ask them what they do with you on the weekends they're here, they always tell me they just sit around and do nothing. If you're not doing anything with them anyway, why shouldn't I get to spend time with them?"

"It's not about that," Mandy fired back. "When I ask them what they do with you, they tell me the same thing. You know how kids are. They always say they are bored and they almost never tell you what they did on any given day. I might let them go if you had something special going on that couldn't be done another time, but you can go to the zoo any weekend they are with you."

"You just want to keep them away from me," Bill argued. "You have to control everything, don't you!"

"Well, I *am* the custodial parent and we agreed on a visitation schedule, so I think we should stick to it, unless there's a real good reason to make an exception. This isn't one," Mandy replied.

"Okay. Let me see the kids so that I can tell them that you won't let them come with me," Bill demanded.

"No, I'll tell them. I don't want you twisting what I said or telling them how I'm keeping you from them," Mandy said.

Bill called out, "Kids! Come here for a minute!" Then he turned to Mandy and said, "I'll remember this the next time you ask to see the kids at a time that's not scheduled."

Flo shook her head at the screen. "It's so sad. I see this kind of scene over and over. Parents agree to a schedule, but one is always trying to change it. The other doesn't want to give in so they constantly argue about it. The unfortunate thing is that most of the time, it's not even about seeing the kids. It's more about control or not giving up ground to the other parent."

Sunday 8:00 am – Competitive Sports

ON THE DREAM CATCHER screen, Brian and Mandy are sitting in a gymnasium where a volleyball game has just finished. As they stand to go down to the floor, Mandy spots Bill and his girlfriend heading towards Jenny. Mandy turned to Brian and said, "I can't stand this! Why is *she* here? She has no right hugging *my* daughter. It's bad enough that I have to see Bill every time one of the kids has a game or something else. Now, I have to put up with that bimbo. I wonder if she even has a brain! Plus, she dresses like a teenager. I mean, look at how short that skirt is and, talk about cleavage! Any more and she'd be putting on a show for all the guys! Brian, are you listening to me?"

Brian snapped his attention back to Mandy and said, "Of course, dear. Well, I guess Bill must feel that she is a part of his family."

"Sure, go ahead, take *his* side!" Mandy snorted. "Maybe it wouldn't be so bad if they were engaged or if I knew it was serious. But, come on, every time Bill moves from one girl to the next, he introduces the kids to them. He shacks up with them for a while or they come over and spend the night when my kids are staying with Bill. What kind of example is he providing? He's had six girlfriends in the last year alone! I don't want my kids to be exposed to that! They need some stability. Who knows what they've seen with *this* bimbo! Probably a heck of a lot more of her than I care to think! If she shows this much in public, what do you think she's showing at home? I wish I had more control over this situation."

Sunday 10:00 am – Wearing Off

FLO TOOK ONE LAST set of vital statistics. Just as she finished, Brian woke up and looked at her. She smiled, "Welcome back, Mr. Walker. How did you sleep?" Brian stared at her as if trying to comprehend the question. Flo continued, "I'm sure it's hard to believe, but you've just finished the 24-hour period on Splitus. Once you feel up to it, you can take a shower and get dressed. After lunch, one of our social workers will be in to discuss your experience."

Post-Treatment Counseling Session
Sunday 1:00 pm

JUST AS BRIAN FINISHED his lunch, a woman walked into his room. "Hello, Mr. Walker, I am Colleen, one of the social workers here at the clinic, and I'd like to spend some time with you discussing your experience, when you're ready."

"I'm not sure I'll ever be completely ready, so I guess now is as good a time as any," Brian responded.

"Great! Then, let's get started. I know this might not be easy but tell me some of the things that you recall about what you saw while under the influence of the Divorce Pill. What do you remember and how did it make you feel?" Colleen asked.

35

"Well, I was surprised by the clarity of everything," Brian cautiously started. "I mean, from the time the visions started until the end, it was as if I was living life as I am today. I thought I would be just observing scenes, kind of like what Scrooge did in *A Christmas Carol*, but that wasn't the case. I was an active participant in every scene and I felt everything that I experienced. I'm not sure that I want anything to do with it!

One part that stands out for me was after Lillie and I decided to divorce. I came over to the house to pick the kids up. I rang the doorbell and Connie came running to the door and opened it. The boys were in the basement and Connie innocently asked me to come in. I didn't think anything of it and stepped inside. Just then, Lillie came around the corner and screamed at me, 'Now, hold on a minute! I didn't invite you inside. You wait out on the porch!' Well, it was then that it hit me that I was not welcome in what was my own home. Things had changed.

Another thing that became clear to me is that I need to discuss the affair with Lillie and give her a chance to share how it made her feel. Although she knows about it, I've been unwilling to confront it. I've taken the position that it's no use. Well, having seen what I did over the last 24 hours, I now have a different perspective. I owe it to her, the kids, and myself to try to work things out.

Now, I don't know for sure whether what I saw in the hallucinations is actually what will happen in my life, but if it is any indication of what waits me in the future, I don't want anything to do with it. It may not be easy going through the pain of admitting to my mistakes and taking responsibility for what I've done, but that doesn't even compare to the pain I would cause Lillie and the kids with a divorce.

I know it's not going to be easy and it may take a long time to heal the brokenness I've caused, but I can't just throw away my family by walking out without trying. Lillie may never forgive me, and we may not be able to get past this, but I have to at least try to make things right. I'll do whatever it takes!"

"That's a good start," Colleen said supportively.

"I couldn't believe the change I saw in Lillie after the divorce," Brian continued. "She became someone I didn't know and did things I would never have expected. I'm glad it was just a hallucination. She is a beautiful, healthy, and vibrant woman who helps others feel better about themselves. To think that she could be thrown into a state of depression deep enough for her to attempt suicide is just beyond my comprehension. I couldn't live with myself if that were to happen. I've put her through a lot of crap in our marriage, yet she's stood beside me through it all. Even when she had the one-night-stand, it was only to get back at me. I was so stupid in trying to put her down for that, when I was the cause of her even doing it. I'm glad that was just a hallucination as well.

I was also surprised at who I became after the divorce. I was a real jerk to Lillie. I didn't treat her with respect, and I manipulated the kids by telling them lies and trying to turn them against her. I don't want to turn into that guy!"

"So, based on what you experienced, how do you look at divorce now?" Colleen asked.

"I think it sucks," Brian responded. "I guess before this experience, I knew that it would be difficult on the kids and that we would all have to make an adjustment, but I had no idea just how much crap was involved. It changed every aspect of our lives. Sure, we would all adjust and make it through, but at what price? I'm not willing to incur the costs. I'm not talking about the financial costs, which could be large. Rather, I'm talking about the toll it will take on Lillie, the kids, me and others in our lives."

"So, when you leave here, what will you do next?" Colleen asked.

"The first thing I'm going to do is go home and hug my wife and kids and tell them how much I've missed them and how much I love them," Brian said. "I am going to commit to them that we will always be a family as long as I have a choice. Then, I will sit down with Lillie and have a long conversation about my experience and tell her that I am willing to do whatever it takes to salvage our marriage."

"Sounds like a good start. Are there any other questions you have for me?" Colleen asked.

Brian smiled. "Just one. May I leave now? I can't wait to start making things right with Lillie."

"Yes, you may," Colleen chuckled. "Just gather up your personal belongings and check out at the nurse's station. Mr. Walker, I wish you all the best in your marriage and I hope that you stay true to your commitment to do whatever it takes. That's what will be needed for your marriage to succeed. Good luck with it all!"

Returning Home

AS BRIAN PULLED INTO his driveway, he paused for a moment to watch John, Peter, and Connie playing in the front yard. He turned off the engine, stepped out of his car and ran over to them. "Hey guys. Come over here and give me a big hug!" As they all ran to Brian, with tears in his eyes he hugged them all tightly in a group-hug and said, "I missed you and I love you more than you'll ever know."

Struggling for air, Connie gasped, "Dad! You've only been gone for a day! I love you too, but I can't breathe."

"Sorry. I just wanted you to know that you mean the world to me." With that, Brian released the kids and they went back to play. He watched them a few minutes longer and then headed into the house.

As he entered through the garage door, Lillie was standing in the kitchen flipping through a cookbook. Brian eagerly went over to her, hugged, and held her tightly for several minutes. Then he paused, looked her in the eye and said, "I love you and I'm so sorry for all the pain I've caused you. I want to work things out and find a way to start over. I want to spend the rest of my life with you. I know that you are the best thing that's ever happened to me."

Lillie was taken back by Brian's sudden show of affection; they had been just tolerating each other for quite some time. Lillie hesitated, "What did they do to you at the clinic? You're not the guy who left here yesterday morning."

"You're right. I'm not the guy who left here yesterday. But, I *am* the guy who fell in love with you and married you 15 years ago. Over the last 24 hours, I got a glimpse into what our future might look like if we were apart, and I didn't like what I saw. Let me tell you what I experienced." The two of them went into the family room and sat down. Brian explained the process, how the Divorce Pill works, and what he saw while under its influence.

"I remember everything clearly right now and I want to share what I saw. It was awful! In the hallucination, I made the decision to divorce. I decided that I wasn't willing to fight for our marriage. I wasn't willing to deal with my failure or to live up to our vows. I wasn't willing to do the work it would take to allow you time to heal. Because of that, our world – yours, the kids and mine – was turned upside down." Brian went on, describing the scenes from the hallucinations as Lillie listened in disbelief.

"That sounds like quite the experience. It seems almost unbelievable," Lillie said quietly.

"I thought so too, but when I talked with the social worker afterwards, she told me that what I experienced was what many people go through when they divorce," Brian explained. "While things might not happen exactly as they did in the hallucination, the situations that we will confront could parallel those. What's important to me is that I don't ever want to experience what I saw. It made me realize just how lucky I am to have you as my wife. You are a perfect match for me! I don't want to throw it all away and I've decided that I am willing to do whatever it takes to make our marriage work. I hope it's not too late. I know I've been a real jerk and that I messed up royally by having the affair with Anita. I am finished screwing around. From this day forward, I vow to be one hundred percent faithful to you, physically and emotionally! You *are* the love of my life and I know that there is nobody out there who can make me feel like you do."

"I don't know whether I can go through this," said Lillie. "I know you feel this way today, but in a year or two or at some point down the road when all of this is just a distant memory, you'll slip away again. I just don't know if I can handle it. I don't know if I can ever trust you again."

Brian reached up to wipe away Lillie's tears. "I guess the question is, are you willing to give it a try?" Brian asked. "Will you give me another chance? Is there some small piece of the love you once had for me remaining? Isn't it worth at least trying? I can tell you that the alternative is not good at all based on what I experienced. Why don't we start slowly, take it a day at a time, and see what happens? The clinic gave me numbers of some good marriage counselors and if you are willing, I'd like to schedule an appointment as soon as we can."

Lillie hesitated.

"Please Lillie, let's give it a try," Brian urged.

"Okay. Go ahead and set it up and let's see where it takes us."

Epilogue

One Year Later

A YEAR AFTER BRIAN spent the night at the clinic under the influence of the Divorce Pill, he scheduled a follow-up appointment with the social worker, Colleen.

"Well, hello Mr. Walker." Colleen greeted Brian as he entered her office.

"Hi Colleen," Brian said as he shook her hand. "I hope you don't mind, but I asked Lillie to join us today. Since my experience last year, we've gone through a lot, and I thought it would be good for you to hear her perspective."

"I don't mind at all. I'm glad you brought her. Pleased to meet you," Colleen said as she shook Lillie's hand. She gestured for them to have a seat. "So Brian, when you left here last year, you said that you were going to take some steps to change your life."

"Yes, and I did," Brian quickly responded. "When I went home that day, Lillie and I had a long talk. Well, actually, I did most of the talking. I filled her in on what I saw while I was at the clinic. I told her how much she meant to me, apologized for my past mistakes, and asked her for a second chance. I honestly don't think she knew what to think at that point, but she agreed to give it a shot. So, we started going to a marriage counselor about a week later."

"I was definitely skeptical," Lillie chimed in. "The way Brian came home and started talking about his experience was hard to believe. It was even harder for me to believe that he would change. We had been at an impasse for so long that I couldn't see any other way out than divorce. Before he left, we were ready to see lawyers. It was that bad. In my mind, I thought that this would be just another time when Brian said he was going to change, but nothing would happen. He had a pattern of doing that in the past. I always ended up feeling stupid and worse for having trusted him. But, even though I was skeptical, something inside me encouraged me to give it one more chance. I have to say that I'm glad I did."

"So, things are better," Colleen reflected.

Lillie continued, "It is amazing what's happened within the last year. Through the marriage counseling, we were able to uncover the reasons why we drifted apart. We learned how Brian's sexual experience before we were married kind of set him up to be unfaithful. I'm sure you know this, but I didn't. The more sexual partners someone has before marriage, the higher the likelihood for infidelity. Plus, there's other baggage that Brian brought into our relationship without knowing it at the time. That doesn't excuse what he did, but it helps us understand at least part of the reason why he was unfaithful. For the first time, Brian accepted responsibility for having the affair. We identified the root causes of our issues and went through inner healing prayer to break free of them. This opened our eyes to how important faith was, not only for emotional healing, but also for our marriage."

"And, we worked out a plan for our marriage with a marriage coach couple. This couple was trained to help married couples like us to move forward in our relationship towards what we wanted out of our relationship, whereas the counselors helped us deal with the past. We set some goals for our life together and the coach couple helped us to stay on track. One of those goals related to our faith. Before Brian's experience with Splitus, faith was a part of our lives, but it was mostly just about going to church and making sure the kids had a religious education. Through our healing and marriage coaching, we learned how important it was for us to grow in faith as individuals and as a couple and put God at the center of our life and marriage. So, we made a commitment to those things.

We started attending church regularly, and we've gone to some marriage seminars that showed us how to better relate to each other and also demonstrated the power of bringing God into our relationship. Now we are both studying the Bible and we pray together almost every day. We pray for each other, for our marriage, for our kids and for other things that are going on in our lives. We have asked God to help us do what we cannot do on our own. It's made a world of difference in our relationship with each other.

It's given us the ability to handle challenges as they've come up. I can't say that our lives are perfect, but we've come to realize that there is no such thing as a perfect marriage. I still have some problems with trust, but I can now see hope and a future with Brian. I haven't had that for a long time!"

"It's hard for me to believe that just a year ago I was ready to throw in the towel," Brian jumped in. "Even on our worst days, I feel closer to Lillie than I ever have before. I am more in love with her and am connected to her in ways that seem surreal. Still, I know that marriage takes work, and we have committed to each other to work on it every day, whether that means sitting down and talking through problems or celebrating something we've accomplished together. For me, it's the difference between *saying* the marriage vows and *living* them."

Lillie nodded as Brian continued. "One of the other things that I've noticed over the last year is that we have grown stronger as a family. I feel closer to the kids and they seem to be happier. I once heard it said that the best gift that a father can give his children is to let them see how much he loves and cherishes their mother. I can testify to the truth of that!"

"It really sounds like you two have made a lot of progress," Colleen said. "I'm glad to see that things are working out for you. It's always a joy for me to see marriages work. Is there any way I can help you?"

"Well, you can pray for us," Brian responded. "Other than that, continue to do the work you are doing here. It would be great if people didn't have to get to the point of needing something like the Divorce Pill, but if our story is anything like others', it can truly be a transformational experience. I'm glad I went through the experience and then chose to stay in my marriage with Lillie."

"So am I," Lillie added.

"I'm happy for both of you and wish you continued success and growth in your marriage. If there's anything I can do to help at any point, please don't hesitate to call me," Colleen stood up to end the session and escorted Lillie and Brian to the door.

Afterword

NOW THAT YOU'VE had a glimpse into what life might be like after divorce, does it make you think twice? I hope so. You may not believe what Brian experienced, but I can tell you it's only the tip of the iceberg! Divorce almost always puts a strain on everyone involved, whether it shows outwardly or not. At some point, the pain surfaces and the damage caused becomes apparent. The issues may not be visible during the brief interactions the ex-husband and ex-wife have with each other after the divorce, but they almost always exist.

They may not be visible in the children. One indicator parents look at are grades, but even a child who is performing well in school may have hidden issues that fester over time and show up later as acting out. Why has there been an increase in the number of children on anti-depressants and teen suicide? Is it possible that at least part of it is caused by what's going on with their parents, or being shuttled back and forth between Mom's and Dad's house? I can't say with certainty, but wonder whether it's an indicator of the impact of divorce on children.

Nobody enters marriage thinking that they will divorce. One thing I've learned it is that love and marriage are choices, and in order for them to be successful, the man and woman need to *choose* to remain faithful, *choose* to work things out, *choose* to stay no matter what, and remain committed through all life's challenges.

I'm not suggesting that there aren't real and legitimate reasons for divorce, such as abuse and repeated infidelity. I'm also not suggesting that blended families don't work out or that some situations may actually be better. But, in the vast majority of cases, divorce is preventable, and when husband and wife choose to work things out, it is better for all involved. Even when all hope seems lost, reconciliation is still possible. It takes time, effort, commitment, outside help, and, in my opinion and experience, being centered on Jesus as our source of wholeness and strength. Studies repeatedly show that most couples who work through their difficulties, even when all hope seemed lost, come out on the other side stronger and more committed, with a happier, more fulfilling relationship.

There are many resources available to couples who are struggling with marriage. Clergy, counselors, and marriage coaches can help couples work through and overcome difficulties. Marriage and relationship education and programs can equip couples with skills needed to increase their chance of success. Books and online information provide additional support.

I encourage you to take advantage of all of these resources and commit to participating in at least one marriage-strengthening program each year.

Staying married takes time and effort, and if you make it a priority, you will gain blessings beyond description. It won't always be easy, but you will have a fulfilling journey with your life partner. May you do all it takes to make your marriage successful, healthy, and lasting, and may you be blessed beyond your wildest expectations!

About the Author

AFTER A 30-YEAR career in pharmaceutical marketing, Doug Bierl turned his attention towards helping to build, restore, and strengthen healthy marriages through professional coaching, training, and writing.

Doug married during college and had four children within seven years. He poured most of his time and energy into advancing in his education and career, largely at the expense of his marriage and family. He didn't invest time in his marriage relationship and drifted apart from his wife. So, fifteen years into the marriage, he decided to end it, not wanting to address the underlying reasons or do the work needed to restore the marriage.

A year after his divorce, Doug met Julaine, whom he married six months later. She was divorced, with two children and so Doug and Julaine blended a family of six children between the ages of 5 and 16. Through the years they experienced many ups and downs. Although all of the children found their way to be productive adults, their journeys were not without a significant amount of pain along the way. Doug and Julaine are happily married and they have learned a lot from their experience, including the importance of investing in the health of their marriage, even and especially when things are going well.

They are intentional about focusing on their marriage and making it a priority in their life.

Doug and Julaine now use their experience and approaches they've been trained and certified in, to work as "Marriage Navigators" to journey with engaged and married couples to help navigate the ups and downs of marriage.

You can learn more at www.ReclaimingWholeness.Life.